First Facts

SUPER SCARY STUFF

SUPER SCARY GHOSTS

BY MEGAN COOLEY PETERSON

CAPSTONE PRESS
a capstone imprint

First Facts are published by Capstone Press,
1710 Roe Crest Drive, North Mankato, Minnesota 56003
www.mycapstone.com

Library of Congress Cataloging-in-Publication Data
Names: Peterson, Megan Cooley, author.
Title: Super scary ghosts / by Megan Cooley Peterson.
Description: North Mankato, Minnesota : First Facts are published by Capstone
    Press, [2017] | Series: First facts. Super scary stuff | Includes
    bibliographical references and index.
Identifiers: LCCN 2015041211
    ISBN 9781515702764 (library binding)
    ISBN 9781515702801 (eBook pdf)
Subjects: LCSH: Ghosts—Juvenile literature.
Classification: LCC BF1461 .P437 2017 | DDC 133.1—dc23
LC record available at http://lccn.loc.gov/2015041211

Editorial Credits
Carrie Braulick Sheely, editor; Kyle Grenz, designer; Svetlana Zhurkin, media researcher;
    Katy LaVigne, production specialist

Photo Credits
Alamy: Rik Hamilton, 21; Getty Images: Apic, 19 (top), Fine Art Photographic/Charles Temple Dix,
11; Library of Congress, 17 (bottom); Newscom: Danita Delimont Photography/Brian Jannsen, 9,
UIG/Underwood Archives, 7, ZUMA Press/Charlie Neuman, 15 (top); Shutterstock: andreiuc88,
cover, CO Leong, 15 (bottom), Everett Historical, 17 (top), jurgenfr, 1, Lario Tus, 5, mary416, 19
(bottom), Robyn Mackenzie, 6; SuperStock: Marsden Archive, 13

Design Elements by Shutterstock

Printed and bound in China.
007702

TABLE OF CONTENTS

BUMP IN THE NIGHT

At a sleepover, you and your friends huddle in sleeping bags. Someone tells a ghost story. Suddenly a cool breeze whisks around the room. You hear strange knocking sounds. Is it a *ghost*?

Do the *spirits* of the dead really walk among us? No matter what you believe, thousands of scary ghost stories exist. Take a deep breath, and prepare to get shivers down your spine!

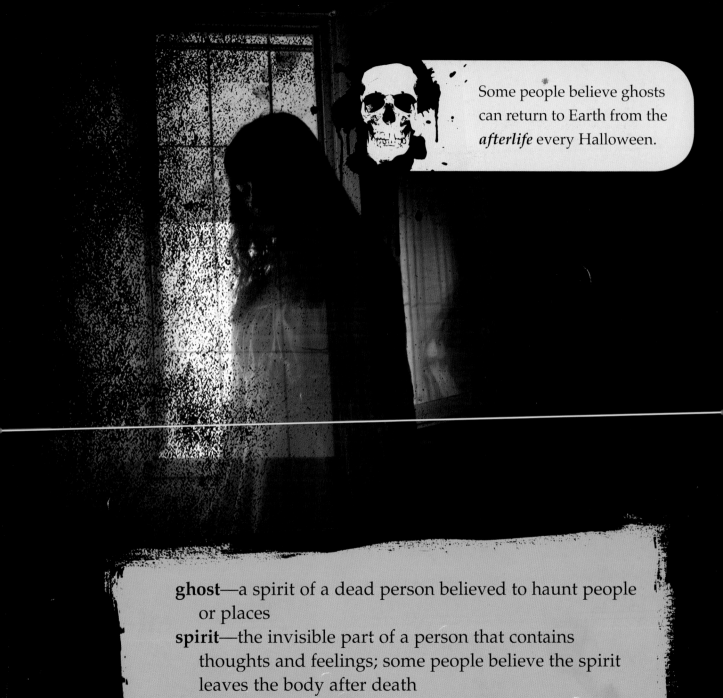

Some people believe ghosts can return to Earth from the *afterlife* every Halloween.

ghost—a spirit of a dead person believed to haunt people
 or places

spirit—the invisible part of a person that contains
 thoughts and feelings; some people believe the spirit
 leaves the body after death

afterlife—the life that some people believe begins when
 a person dies

A BANJO-PLAYING GHOST

In the 1920s Al Capone was a feared leader of the Chicago *Mafia*. In 1931 he was arrested and later sent to Alcatraz prison. While in prison, he played the banjo in a band.

Capone died at his home in 1947. But his ghost might have stuck around at Alcatraz. Workers at the prison say ghostly banjo music plays in Capone's old cell. Others have heard banjo music in the showers where Capone practiced.

The Mafia began in Sicily, Italy. In the late 1800s, members of this crime group came to the United States. Over time a separate Mafia formed in the United States. It still exists today.

Mafia—a criminal organization that controls illegal activities over a large area

EMILY'S BRIDGE

Beware of the Gold Brook Bridge in Stowe, Vermont. According to *legend*, a woman died on the bridge in the 1800s. Her name was Emily. At night her ghost is said to haunt those who cross it. People say Emily's ghost hits cars and scratches visitors. Ghostly footsteps and screams have been heard on the bridge. Some people have reported a white mist shaped like a woman near the bridge.

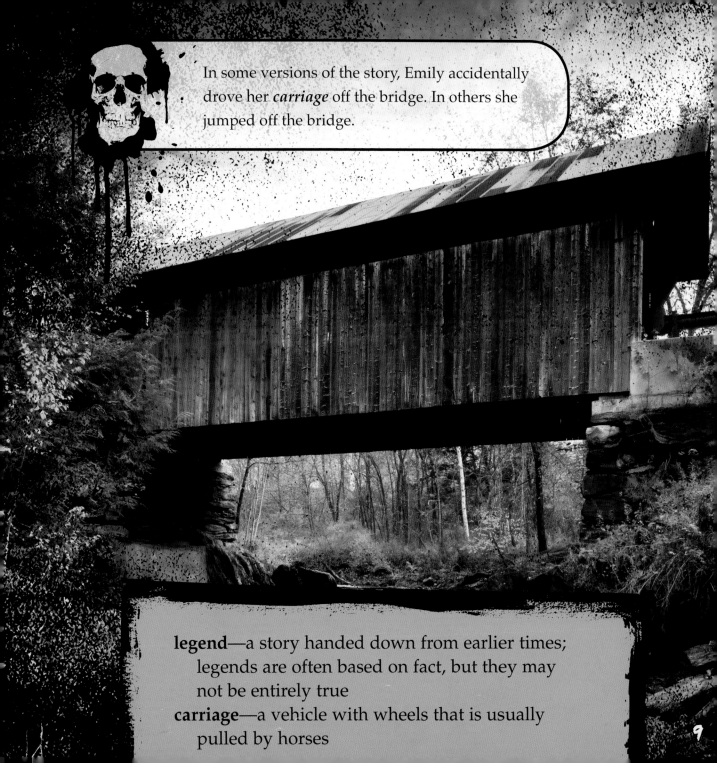

In some versions of the story, Emily accidentally drove her *carriage* off the bridge. In others she jumped off the bridge.

legend—a story handed down from earlier times; legends are often based on fact, but they may not be entirely true

carriage—a vehicle with wheels that is usually pulled by horses

A DOOMED SHIP

Sailors have feared the *Flying Dutchman* for hundreds of years. Legend says the ship sank sailing around the southern tip of Africa in 1680. It dragged the captain and crew to their watery graves. Now the ghost ship is doomed to roam the seas forever. Swift disaster is said to come to anyone who sees the ship.

The *Flying Dutchman* appeared in Disney's *Pirates of the Caribbean* movies.

THE HAUNTED HALL

Walk carefully on the grand staircase of Raynham Hall in England. You may meet a spirit called the Brown Lady. It is thought to be the ghost of Lady Dorothy Walpole. She lived at the hall during the 1700s.

Wearing a brown dress, her ghost floats down the stairs. People say the ghost has black holes where its eyes should be.

A Mysterious Photo

A famous 1936 photo of the grand staircase shows a misty figure. Some people think it shows the Brown Lady. They say the photo proves ghosts are real. But *skeptics* say the camera's film produced a *double exposure*. Others say a smudge on the camera lens created the ghostly shape.

skeptic—a person who questions things that other people believe in

double exposure—a photography method in which two photographs are taken on the same piece of film

13

HAUNTING AT HOTEL DEL CORONADO

In 1892 Kate Morgan checked into room 302 at the Hotel Del Coronado in San Diego, California. She died of a gunshot wound there five days later. But some say she never left.

Visitors and staff say Kate's ghost still haunts the hotel. People report foul smells and flickering lights. TVs turn on and off by themselves. Several guests have reported seeing a ghostly woman in old-fashioned clothing.

According to a 2013 poll, 42 percent of Americans believe in ghosts. In Great Britain, 52 percent of people say ghosts are real.

A PRESIDENTIAL GHOST

In December 1799 George Washington became ill. The former U.S. president died in bed at his home in Mount Vernon, Virginia. In 1806 politician Josiah Quincy III visited Mount Vernon. He later claimed to have seen Washington's ghost in the former president's bedroom.

Other former presidents are said to haunt the White House. Witnesses have seen the ghosts of Abraham Lincoln and Andrew Jackson.

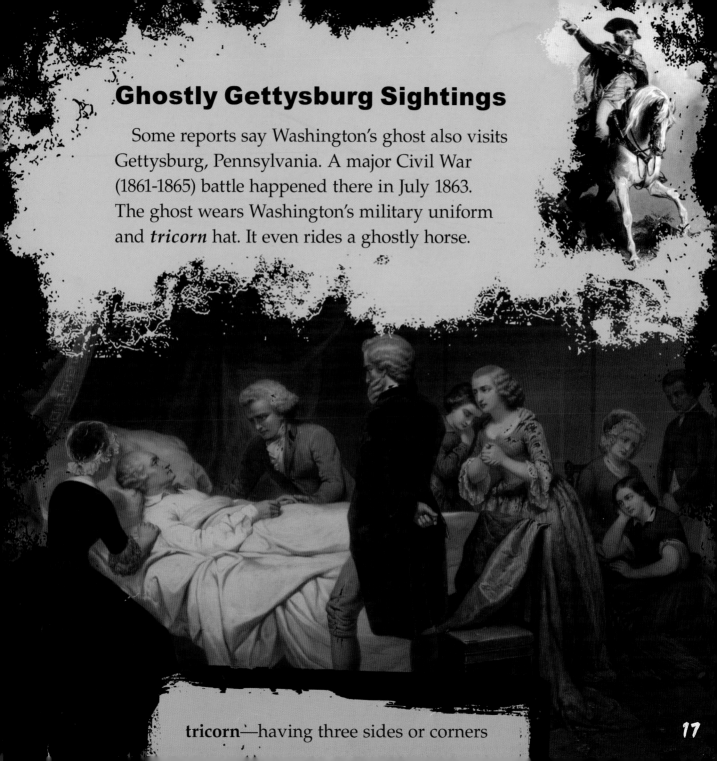

Ghostly Gettysburg Sightings

Some reports say Washington's ghost also visits Gettysburg, Pennsylvania. A major Civil War (1861-1865) battle happened there in July 1863. The ghost wears Washington's military uniform and *tricorn* hat. It even rides a ghostly horse.

tricorn—having three sides or corners

THE SCREAMING LADY

According to legend, *royal* ghosts haunt Hampton Court Palace in England. Catherine Howard is one of its most famous ghosts. In 1541 Catherine's husband, King Henry VIII, had her locked in the palace. She ran through the palace's *gallery*, screaming for help.

Today visitors report hearing a woman screaming in the gallery. Some say they have seen Catherine's ghost being dragged through the gallery.

In 1999 a woman fainted in the gallery. Thirty minutes later another woman fainted in the exact same spot.

royal—having to do with a king or queen
gallery—a place where paintings, sculptures, and other works of art are on display

THE NAMELESS THING

A fearsome ghost may haunt
50 Berkeley Square in London. Called
the Nameless Thing, it appeared in one
of the mansion's bedrooms in the 1800s.
At least one person died mysteriously
while staying in the room. Another person
staying in the room appeared to have
suffered from *shock*. She died the next day.

Like all ghosts, the Nameless Thing may
or may not be real. But you might want to
sleep with the lights on … just in case.

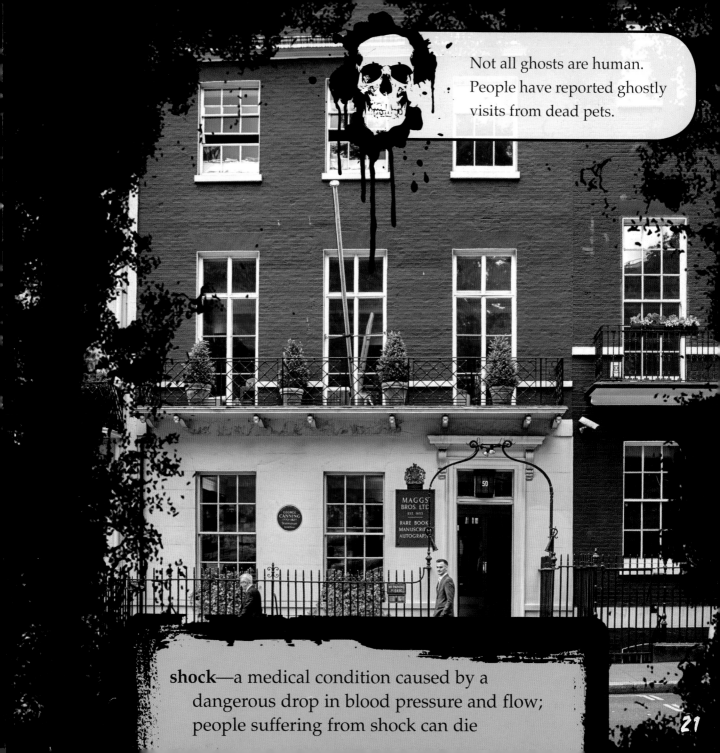

Not all ghosts are human. People have reported ghostly visits from dead pets.

shock—a medical condition caused by a dangerous drop in blood pressure and flow; people suffering from shock can die

GLOSSARY

afterlife (AF-tur-lyfe)—the life that some people believe begins when a person dies

carriage (KAYR-ij)—a vehicle with wheels that is usually pulled by horses

double exposure (DUH-bul ik-SPO-zhur)—a photography method in which two photographs are taken on the same piece of film

gallery (GAL-ur-ee)—a place where paintings, sculptures, and other works of art are on display

ghost (GOHST)—a spirit of a dead person believed to haunt people or places

legend (LEJ-uhnd)—a story handed down from earlier times; legends are often based on fact, but they may not be entirely true

Mafia (MAH-fee-uh)—a criminal organization that controls illegal activities over a large area

royal (ROY-uhl)—having to do with a king or queen

shock (SHOK)—a medical condition caused by a dangerous drop in blood pressure and flow

skeptic (SKEP-tik)—someone who questions things that other people believe in

spirit (SPIHR-it)—the invisible part of a person that contains thoughts and feelings; some people believe the spirit leaves the body after death

tricorn (TRY-corn)—having three sides or corners

READ MORE

Collins, Terry. *Scooby-Doo! And the Truth Behind Ghosts.* Unmasking Monsters with Scooby-Doo. North Mankato, Minn.: Capstone Press, 2015.

Hamilton, S. L. *Ghost Hunting.* Xtreme Adventure. Minneapolis: ABDO Publishing Company, 2014.

Raij, Emily. *Ghosts of the Rich and Famous.* Spooked! North Mankato, Minn.: Capstone Press, 2016.

INTERNET SITES

FactHound offers a safe, fun way to find Internet sites related to this book. All of the sites on FactHound have been researched by our staff.

Here's all you do:

Visit *www.facthound.com*

Type in this code: 9781515702764

Super-cool stuff! Check out projects, games and lots more at
www.capstonekids.com

INDEX